TRILLIONS OF TREES

A COUNTING AND PLANTING BOOK

KURT CYRUS

Christy Ottaviano Books

Henry Holt and Company • New York

Henry Holt and Company, *Publishers since 1866*
Henry Holt® is a registered trademark of Macmillan Publishing Group, LLC
120 Broadway, New York, NY 10271
mackids.com

Library of Congress Cataloging-in-Publication Data
Names: Cyrus, Kurt, author, illustrator.
Title: Trillions of trees / Kurt Cyrus.
Description: First edition. | New York : Henry Holt and Company, 2021. | "Christy Ottaviano Books." | Audience: Ages 3–6. | Audience: Grades K–1.
| Summary: "Grab a shovel and get ready to plant some trees! From poplars to pines, alder, apple, peach, and plum, this rhyming story introduces the concept of orders of magnitude and celebrates the importance of planting different trees and preserving diverse ecosystems. Nurturing a new sapling is one of the first steps in growing hundreds, millions, even trillions of trees" —Provided by publisher.
Identifiers: LCCN 2020020579 | ISBN 9781250229076 (hardcover)
Subjects: CYAC: Stories in rhyme. | Trees—Fiction. | Counting.
Classification: LCC PZ8.3.C997 Tr 2021 | DDC [E]—dc23
LC record available at https://lccn.loc.gov/2020020579

Our books may be purchased in bulk for promotional, educational, or business use. Please contact your local bookseller or the Macmillan Corporate and Premium Sales Department at (800) 221-7945 ext. 5442 or by email at MacmillanSpecialMarkets@macmillan.com.

First edition, 2021 / Book design by Mike Burroughs
Printed in China by RR Donnelley Asia Printing Solutions Ltd., Dongguan City, Guangdong Province.
10 9 8 7 6 5 4 3 2 1

For my tree-planting brother Steve

We never meant to plant a tree.
We wanted something small.
"A trillium!" my sister said.
And so she placed a call.

Polly's
PLANT Pavilion
Spring

Trillium

"I'd like to buy a trillium, please,"
said Lizzie to the man.
He *thought* she said "a **trillion** trees."
That's how it all began.

"A **trillion** trees?" the salesman said.
"We'll do our very best.
I'll send a **thousand** right away
and order up the rest!"

Trees!
Trees!
Trees!
They knocked us to our knees.
In boxes, bags, and burlap rags—
Trees!
Trees!
Trees!

Our shovel couldn't hack it.
We bought a couple more,
and then we started digging
like we've never dug before.

Dig!
Dig!
Dig!
A filbert and a fig.
A beech, a gum,
a peach, a plum.

Dig!
Dig!
Dig!

We dug and dug. The ground was hard.
We stuck a **hundred** in our yard.

Trees!
  Trees!
    Trees!
Another **hundred**, please.
All up and down the streets of town.
    Trees!
      Trees!
        Trees!

A county park! The perfect place!
(We asked permission, just in case.)
Along the trails and all around—
another **hundred** in the ground!

Dig! Dig! Dig!
These apple trees are big.
An orchard goes for rows and rows.
Dig! Dig! Dig!

Plant a windbreak. Poplars! Pines!
Stretch them out in perfect lines.

Plant another **hundred** trees.

Alder, ash, and willow, please.

Shade a river. Shade a pool.

Fish prefer their water cool.

Also good?
Cottonwood.

"Trilliums!" my sister cheers.

I just groan and plug my ears.

Spruce and hemlock. Cedar, too.
A fir for her, a yew for you.
And look! Sequoia! These are great!
They're tiny now . . .

but just you wait!

Chop the ground. Pry it back.
Pull a seedling from your sack.
One by **one**, the trees return
to heal the scarring from a burn.

Here the slope is very steep.
Plant a **hundred**, not too deep.
Mountain hemlock. Sugar pine.
Douglas-fir is also fine.

Hold, roots, hold!
Keep the slope controlled.
Grip that mud. Stop that flood.
Hold, roots, hold!

They build the soil. They clean the air.
They work their wonders everywhere.
Billions.
Trillions!
Trees galore.
And thanks to us—a **thousand** more!

We're out of gas. The car is dead.
We'll have to use our feet instead.

Ow.
  Ow.
    Ow.
We're bruised and blistered now.
Our knees are weak. Our elbows creak.
      Ow.
        Ow.
          Ow.

A truck is in the driveway.
It's Polly's Plant Pavilion . . .

Grab
a tree.

It's going to be
a long way to a **trillion.**